Contents

A Stormy Night

One stormy night, a little girl named Sarah was home alone. She was in her room, reading a book by the light of a lamp when she heard a noise coming from downstairs. It sounded like someone was walking around in the living room.

Sarah was scared, but she didn't want to be a scaredy-cat. She decided to go downstairs and see what was making the noise. As she walked down the stairs, the noise got louder and louder. It sounded like someone was definitely walking around in the living room.

Sarah got to the bottom of the stairs and peeked into the living room. There was no one there. She looked around the room, but there was nothing out of place. She was just about to go back upstairs when she heard the noise again.

This time, it sounded like it was coming from the kitchen. Sarah walked into the kitchen, but there was no one there, either. She looked around, but everything was in its place.

Suddenly, she heard the noise again. This time, it sounded like it was coming from outside. Sarah went to the window and looked out, but there was no one there. She was just about to go back upstairs when she heard a voice. It sounded like it was coming from upstairs.

Sarah's heart was pounding in her chest. She didn't want to go upstairs, but she knew she had to. Slowly, she walked up the stairs. The noise got louder and louder as she got closer to her bedroom.

Sarah's bedroom door was closed. She put her hand on the doorknob and took a deep breath. Then she turned the knob and walked into the room. There was no one there. Sarah was relieved.

She was about to go back downstairs when she heard the noise again. This time, it sounded like it was coming from inside her closet. Sarah's heart skipped a beat.

She didn't want to go into the closet, but she knew she had to. She took a deep breath and opened the door. There was no one there.

Sarah was about to close the door when she saw something moving inside the closet. She froze in fear. Then, out of the shadows, a ghost appeared.

Sarah screamed and ran out of the room. She ran downstairs and out of the house. She didn't stop running until she got to her friend's house. She pounded on the door, and when her friend answered, she burst into tears.

"Sarah, what's wrong?" her friend asked. "There's a ghost in my house!" Sarah cried. Her friend didn't believe her at first, but when Sarah told her what she had seen, she believed her. The two girls went back to Sarah's house, but the ghost was gone. Sarah never saw it again, but she always remembered that scary night.

****

Revenge Story

One grey day, a small girl named Ruby was playing in her backyard when she saw something move in the bushes. She went to investigate and found a small white rabbit. The rabbit was shaking and looked very scared. Ruby picked up the rabbit and held it close, trying to comfort it.

Suddenly, the rabbit turned into a ghost! The ghost was transparent and had a scary face. It floated in the air and started to speak in a deep, booming voice.

"I am the ghost of the White Rabbit," the ghost said. "I haunt this house and everyone who lives here. I will never rest until I have my revenge!"

The ghost then floated away into the house. Ruby ran into the house to tell her parents what had happened.

The family was very scared and decided to move out of the house the next day. They never found out what the ghost was revengeful about, but they were glad to be rid of it.

****

A Brave Girl Stroy

It was a dark and stormy night. The kind of night where you would hear things going bump in the night. The wind was howling, and the rain was coming down in sheets. The kind of night that made you want to curl up in a ball under the covers and hope that the morning would come quickly. But there was one little girl who was not afraid of the dark or of the storm. In fact, she loved them both.

She loved the way the lightning lit up the sky and the way the thunder made her whole house shake. This little girl had a secret. She knew that when the storm was at its worst, the ghosts would

come out to play. She had seen them before, peeking out from
behind the trees or flying high above the rooftops.

Tonight, she was determined to see them again. So, she put on
her raincoat and boots and went outside. The wind was so strong
that it nearly blew her away, but she held on tight to the fence
and made her way to the tree in the middle of the yard.

She climbed up high into the branches and waited. Soon, she saw
the first ghost. It was a small one, with a pale face and a long,
flowing dress. It floated slowly through the air, stopping every so
often to look around.

The little girl watched as the ghost floated from one house to the
next. She followed it with her eyes until it disappeared into the

darkness. Suddenly, she felt something cold and wet touch her hand.

She looked down and saw a second ghost, this one much larger than the first. It had a big, round head and two big, black eyes. It was staring right at her! The little girl was so scared that she started to shake.

But she didn't take her eyes off the ghost. She was too fascinated by it. Eventually, the ghost floated away and the little girl climbed down from the tree. She was cold and wet, but she didn't care. She had seen the ghosts and that was all that mattered.

As she walked back to her house, she couldn't help but smile. She knew that she would be back out tomorrow night, ready to see what other ghosts she could find.

****

A Crying Ghost

One autumn night, a group of kids was playing in the park. It was getting late, but they didn't want to go home. Suddenly, they heard a noise. It sounded like someone was crying.

They followed the noise until they came to a small, old house. The windows were boarded up and the front door was hanging open. The kids were scared, but they decided to go inside.

They only made it a few steps before they were surrounded by ghosts. The ghosts were crying and moaning, and they looked really sad.

The kids tried to run, but the ghosts were too fast. They were trapped! The ghosts started to speak, and the kids realized that they were trying to tell them something. They were trying to warn the kids about something that was going to happen.

But before they could finish, the ghosts were gone. The kids were left alone in the dark, cold house. They didn't know what to do, so they decided to go home. But they knew they would never forget what happened that night. And they would never go near that house again.

******

The Lost Treasure

One night a little girl was in her bed when she heard a noise coming from outside her window. She got out of bed to see what it was, and she saw a ghost! The ghost was a friendly one, and he told her that he was looking for a lost treasure.

He said that he had been searching for it for a long time, but he couldn't find it. The little girl asked the ghost where he thought the treasure might be. The ghost said that he didn't know, but he was going to keep looking until he found it.

The little girl told the ghost that she would help him look for the treasure. So the two of them searched the house from top to bottom.

They looked in all the rooms and under all the furniture. But they couldn't find the treasure. The ghost was getting discouraged, but the little girl was still determined to help him. She said, "Let's go outside and look around.

Maybe the treasure is hidden somewhere in the garden." So they went outside, and they looked everywhere. They looked in the bushes and under the trees. But they still couldn't find the treasure.

The ghost was ready to give up, but the little girl said, "I know where the treasure is! Follow me!" She led the ghost to a small shed in the corner of the garden. The door was locked, but the little girl had the key.

She opened the door and went inside. And there, in the corner, was the lost treasure! The ghost was so happy, and he thanked the little girl for her help. Then he flew away into the night.

******

Ghosts Are Real

Do you believe in ghosts? I used to think they were make-believe, like the monsters under my bed or the witches in my closet. But I was wrong. Ghosts are real, and they're not always the stuff of nightmares.

Take, for example, the spirit of my great-grandmother, who passed away when I was just a baby. After she died, my mother would often say she could feel her presence in the house. And on more than one occasion, I've been woken up in the middle of the night by the sound of her rocking chair creaking back and forth in the nursery.

It's not always scary when ghosts visit. Sometimes, they just want to let us know they're still around. They might move a vase from one side of the room to the other or turn on a light when we're in the dark. And if you're really lucky, you might even get a chance to talk to them.

I was about 10 years old when I first saw a ghost. It was late at night, and I was trying to go to sleep, when I suddenly felt someone watching me. I sat up in bed and looked around, but there was nobody there.

Then I felt a tap on my shoulder, and when I turned around, I saw a lady standing next to me. She was wearing a long white dress and had a kind face.

"Hello, dear," she said. "I'm sorry if I startled you. I just wanted to let you know that I'm here, and I'll always be watching over you."

Then she was gone, and I was alone in my room again. But I didn't feel scared. I felt comforted, knowing that my great-grandmother was with me.

If you've ever seen a ghost, or felt a presence in your home, then you know they're real. And the next time you see one, don't be afraid. They just might have a message for you.

******

A School Boy

One day a boy was walking home from school and he saw a ghost. The ghost was a mean-looking one too. The boy was so scared that he ran all the way home.

Once he got home, he told his mom what he had seen. His mom said that it was just his imagination and that there was no such thing as ghosts. The boy didn't believe her.

That night, when the boy went to bed, he heard a noise coming from his closet.

He slowly got out of bed and slowly opened the door to his closet. And there was the ghost! The boy screamed and the ghost disappeared.

The next day, the boy went to school and told his friends what had happened. They all laughed at him and said that he was just making this story. The boy knew that they were wrong and that ghosts were real.

From that day on, the boy was never afraid of ghosts again. In fact, he even started to like them.

*****

Phillips and Emily's Stormy Night

It was a dark and stormy night. Phillip and his little sister, Emily, were home alone. Their parents had gone out to dinner and a movie. Phillip was watching TV in the living room and Emily was in her bedroom, reading a book.

Suddenly, they heard a loud crash. It sounded like something had hit the house. Phillip and Emily ran to see what it was. They found a big hole in the wall of the living room. And there was a ghost in their house!

The ghost was a scary-looking man with a long, white beard. He was wearing a black cape and carrying a lantern. He floated into the room and hovered over the hole in the wall.

"I'm here to haunt you!" the ghost said in a deep, booming voice.

Emily started to cry. Phillip was so scared he couldn't move.

The ghost laughed. Then he reached into his lantern and pulled out a sheet of paper. He unrolled it and held it up for Phillip and Emily to see.

"This is my ghost contract," the ghost said. "It says that I can haunt you for three nights. And if you don't do what I say, I'll haunt you forever!"

The ghost laughed again. Then he blew out his lantern and vanished into the darkness. After Phillip and Emily's parents come, they say what happened to them. Then they decide to leave this home forever.

*****

Emily's Dairy

One evening, a group of kids was sitting around a campfire, telling ghost stories. One of the kids, a little girl named Olivia, said she had the most extreme ghost story ever.

Olivia's family had just moved into a new house, and she was excited to explore. One day, she went into the attic and found an old box. Inside the box were some old toys and a diary.

The diary was written in a language Olivia couldn't understand, but she could read the name on the front: "Emily."

Olivia took the diary back to her room and started to read it. The diary told the story of a little girl named Emily, who lived in the house Olivia's family now lived in.

Emily was a very happy girl, One day; her family was killed in a fire. Emily also died in the fire.

Olivia was so scared after reading the diary she didn't want to go into the attic ever again. But one night, she heard strange noises coming from the attic. Olivia was too scared to go up and investigate, so she called her mom.

Olivia's mom went into the attic and found Emily's ghost! Emily's ghost was very sad and scared, and she asked Olivia's mom to help her. Olivia's mom promised to help Emily, and she told Olivia never to go into the attic again.

Olivia never goes into the attic again, but she still thinks about Emily's ghost. She knows that Emily is at peace now, and she's glad she was able to help her.

******

Nail, Emily & Alone Home

It was a dark and stormy night. Nail and his little sister, Emily, were home alone. Their parents had gone to a party and wouldn't be back until late. Nail was 10 years old and Emily was only 6. The power had gone out earlier in the evening, so the house was dark.

Nail had lit some candles and they were huddled together on the couch, trying to stay warm. Suddenly, they heard a noise coming from upstairs. It sounded like someone was walking around. "Emily, stay here," Nail said. He grabbed a candle and started up the stairs. The noise got louder as he got closer to the source.

It was definitely coming from their parent's bedroom. Nail slowly opened the door and peeked inside. What he saw was definitely not human.

There was a figure, all in black, standing in the middle of the room. It was about 7 feet tall and very thin. It had long, black hair that flowed around its face. And its eyes... its eyes were glowing red.

Nail was frozen in place, too scared to move. The figure started moving towards him, floating just above the ground. It reached out a hand and Nail felt himself being lifted off the ground.

He couldn't scream, he couldn't move. He was completely paralyzed.

The figure carried him over to the bed and laid him down. Then it reached out and touched his forehead. Nail felt a cold sensation spreading through his body. He could feel himself being pulled out of his body. He could see himself lying on the bed, his eyes wide open but unseeing. The figure was now standing over him, looking down at him.

Nail could see the red eyes staring at him, cold and emotionless. Then he felt himself being drawn into those eyes... and everything went black. When Nail woke up, he was lying in his bed.

It was morning and the sun was shining in through the window. He sat up, rubbing his eyes. He couldn't believe what had happened. It had to have been a dream. But then he saw the black hair on his pillow. And the red eyes are staring at him from the mirror.

$$* * * * * *$$

<u>A Little Girl Who Loved Ghosts</u>

Once upon a time, there was a little girl who loved ghosts. She would read stories about them, and watch movies that had them in it. She even had a few ghost friends that she would talk to.

One day, she found a book about a ghost that lived in a haunted house. The little girl loved the book so much that she decided to go to the house to see if she could find the ghost.

When she got to the house, she saw the ghost! The ghost was floating around in the air, and he was see-through. The little girl was so excited that she started talking to the ghost.

They talked for a while, and the ghost told her about the other ghosts that lived in the house.

The little girl was so fascinated by the ghost story that she decided to go back home and tell her mom about it.

Then she said everything about the ghost house to her mom, but her mother said don't go there next time. After that she didn't go there anytime.

******

Someone Still In the House

It was a dark and stormy night. William and his sister, Sophia, were home alone. They were in their room, playing with their toys, when they heard a noise. It sounded like something was moving around downstairs. "What was that?" William asked.

"I don't know," Sophia said. "Maybe it's mommy."

They both went to the door and listened. They could hear footsteps. They were definitely coming up the stairs!

"It's not mommy," William said. "She would have called out to us."

"Then who is it?" Sophia asked.

There was a knock on their door. They both froze.

"Who is it?" William called out.

"It's me," a voice said. "Your neighbor, Mrs. Johnson."

"What do you want?" William asked.

"I just wanted to make sure that you guys are okay," she said. "I saw your lights were still on and I know your parents are out of town."

"We're fine," William said. "You can go now."

"Are you sure?" she asked. "I don't mind staying here with you until your parents get home."

"We're sure," William said. "Goodnight."

He closed the door and locked it.

"That was weird," Sophia said.

"I know," William said. "But she's gone now. Let's go back to playing."

They went back to their room and tried to forget about what had happened. But it was hard to forget. Because they both knew that someone was still in the house with them.

******

A Small Boy Summer Evening

One summer evening a small boy was playing in his backyard when he heard a noise coming from the bushes.

He slowly approached the bushes and peeked through to see a ghost! The ghost was a scary-looking man with long black hair and a white sheet covering his body.

The boy was so frightened that he ran into the house and hid under his bed. He could hear the ghost outside, moaning and groaning.

The boy was so scared that he didn't come out from under the bed until morning. When he finally emerged, the ghost was gone and he never saw it again.

But he always remembered that summer evening when he had a close encounter with a real ghost!

******

Kely's Story

One night, a group of kids were sitting around a campfire, telling scary stories. One of the kids, a little girl named Kely, said she knew a really scary story about a ghost.

Kely's story went like this:

There was once a family who lived in a house that was haunted by a ghost.

The ghost was a mean spirit who would haunt the family, making strange noises and moving things around.

The family was terrified of the ghost and did everything they could to avoid it.

One night, the father of the family was home alone and he heard a ghost haunting the house.

The father grabbed a shotgun and went to confront the ghost. He shot the ghost and it disappeared.

The family was relieved that the ghost was gone but then strange things started happening in the house.

The father would find his clothes mysteriously moved around, the doors would slam shut by themselves, and they would hear strange noises coming from the attic.

The family realized that the ghost was still haunting them and they were terrified. They eventually moved out of the house and never came back.

Kely's story was so scary that the other kids were scared too. They all agreed that it was the best scary story they had ever heard.

******

A Little Girl

Once upon a time, there was a little girl who lived in a big house all by herself. She was very lonely and always wanted to make friends. One day, she saw a little girl in a white dress playing in the garden.

The little girl in the white dress looked at her she was so scary but the little girl doesn't afraid. She went up to her and asked if she wanted to be friends. The white dress girl said yes and they played together every day.

One day, the little girl in the white dress said she had to go home and she would come back the next day. She never came back. The little girl was very sad and missed her friend.

One night, she heard a knock on her window. She got out of bed and went to the window. There was the little girl in the white dress! She was so happy to see her friend again. They hugged each other and the little girl in the white dress said she would never leave her friend alone again.

******

Brother & Sister In Alone Home

It was a dark and stormy night. Mehedi and his sister, Jerin, were home alone. Jerin was in her room, reading a book. Mehedi was in his room, playing a video game.

Suddenly, they heard a noise. It sounded like something was moving around downstairs. They both got scared and ran into Jerin's room. They hid under the covers together and tried to make themselves as small as possible.

They heard footsteps coming up the stairs. They were getting closer and closer to Jerin's room.

The doorknob started to turn and the door slowly opened. A figure was standing in the doorway. It was a scary ghost!

The ghost floated into the room and came closer to the bed. Mehedi and Jerin were so scared that they couldn't move. The ghost reached out its hand and touched Jerin's hair. Then it turned to Mehedi and started to strangle him!

Mehedi and Jerin were both terrified. They thought they were going to die. But then, just as suddenly as it had appeared, the ghost vanished. They were both safe. After this day they never saw the ghost.

*****

A Friendly Ghost

One day, a group of kids were playing in the park when they saw a ghost. The ghost was very scary and the kids ran away.

The next day, the kids came back to the park and saw the ghost again. This time, the ghost was friendly and asked the kids to play with him.

The kids were scared at first, but then they realized that the ghost was just like them and they had a lot of fun playing together.

*****

www.ingramcontent.com/pod-product-compliance
Lightning Source LLC
Chambersburg PA
CBHW040927110726
48006CB00001B/100